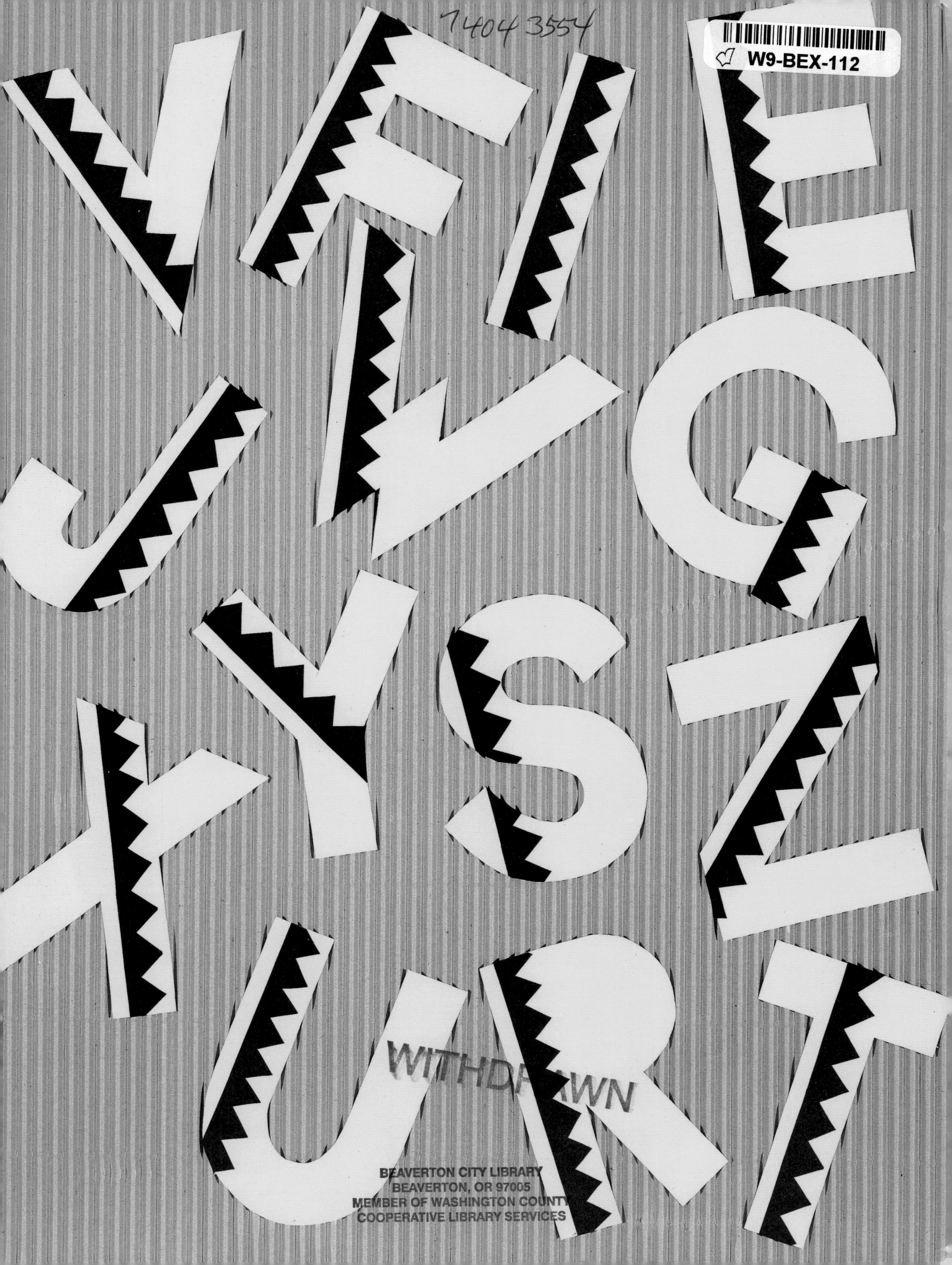

MICHAEL ROBERTS
FOREWORD BY IMAN
THE JUNGLE ABC
CALLAWAY
New York • 2017

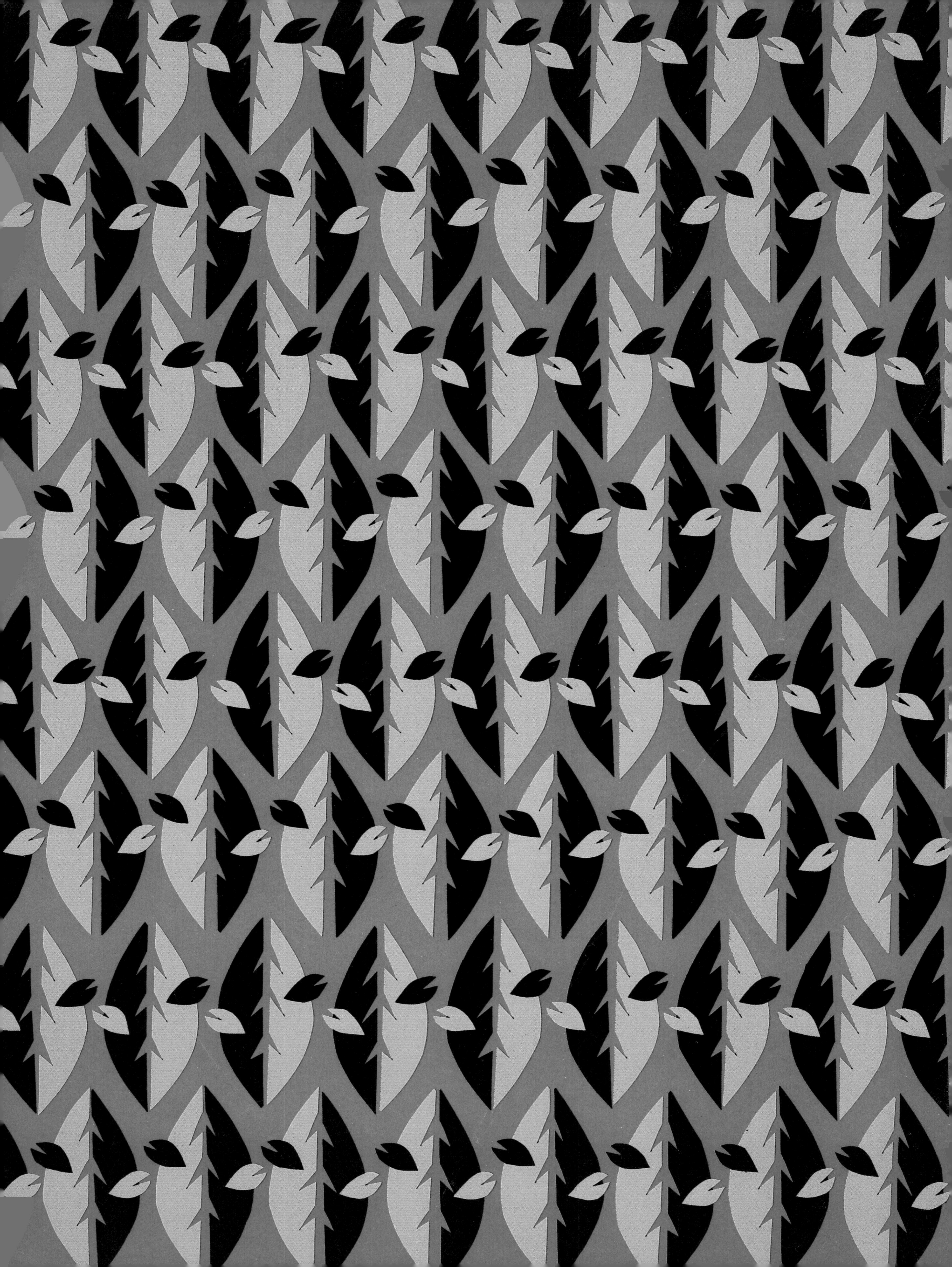

THE JUNGLE WAY
BY NIGHT
AND DAY
IS FULL OF
CRIES
AND AMBER
EYES
WHILE ZULUS
PRANCE
IN
SNAKE-LIKE DANCE
TO
GROOVES HYPNOTIC
QUITE
EXOTIC

For many, the mystery of the African jungle sets it apart as the world's most distant and distinct place — geographically and imaginatively. Just like one of its most popular inhabitants, the crocodile, the African jungle lies languidly in the waters of the world, too fierce to be reckoned with, too intriguing to be ignored.

I was raised in Africa's Somalia, a sub-Saharan land of harsh, sunbaked rock and sand. Somalia was once known as the Horn of Africa for the way it proudly flaunts itself from the rest of the continent, pushing away to cool itself in the sultry waters of the Indian Ocean and the Gulf of Aden. Still, the distant jungle was as much a part of my interior as the arid plains of Somalia were a part of my exterior. In Africa, we are all comprised of that which comprises the total land.

When I left Africa to become a fashion model in America, the spirit of the jungle was carried along with me. On the runway, the tigress inspired my every step; the graceful, erect arch of the giraffe formed my posture; I acknowledged the audience with the same lazy indifference with which the cheetah would acknowledge me.

The jungle is the nighttime of Africa. True, the African sun beats down daily upon this emerald lung, yet it is permanent nighttime within the jungle's depths of twisting vines and sluggish rivers and magnificent wildlife. Just like nighttime, the jungle is all enveloping. Many mistake "jungle" to mean dangerous and menacing. This is not true. Indeed, there are elements of danger in the jungle, but these dangers exist only for intruders who exploit the harmony of its community. Left to itself, the jungle is a perfectly functioning organ, sustaining life for the rest of the body Africa.

— IMAN

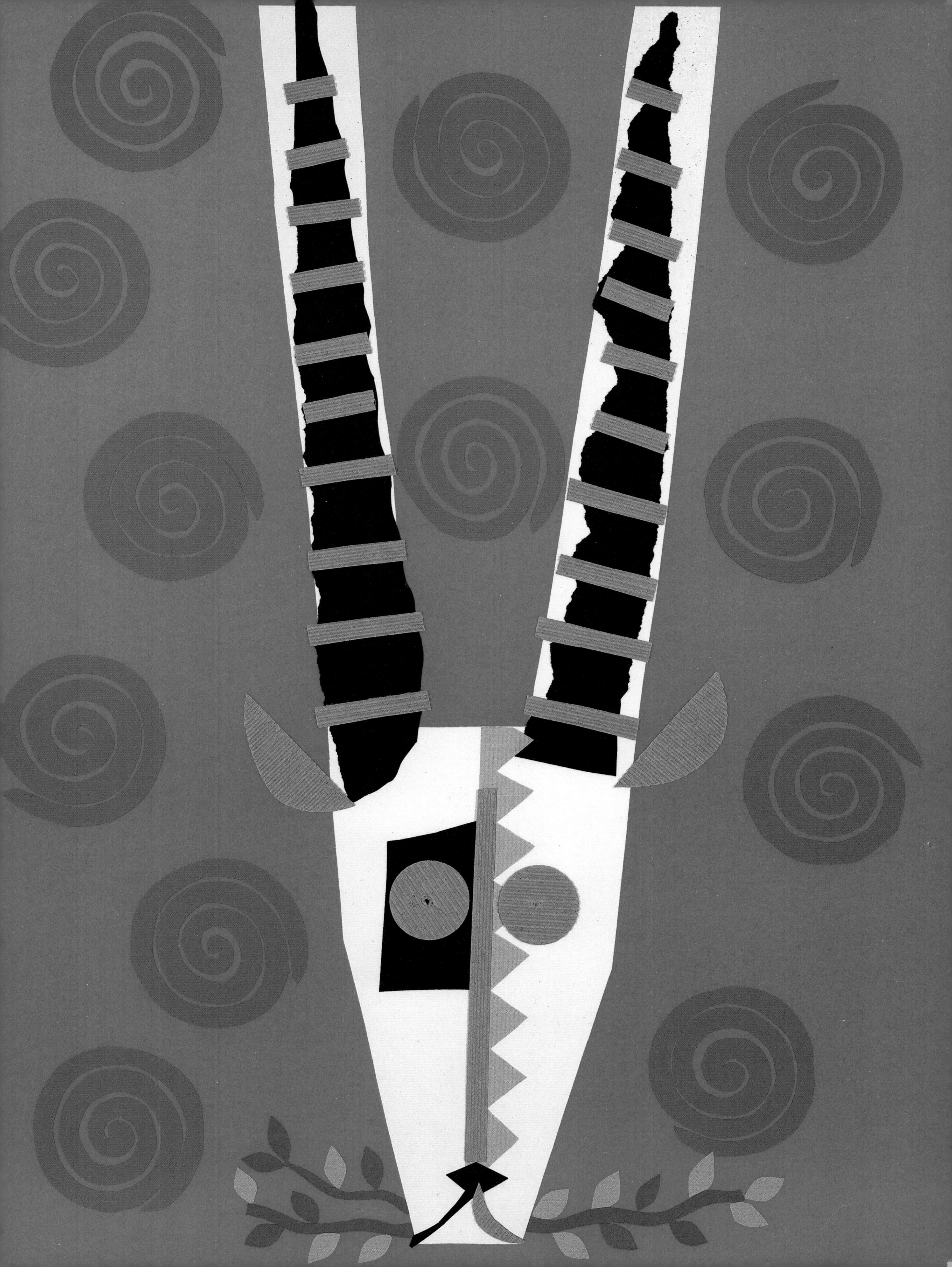

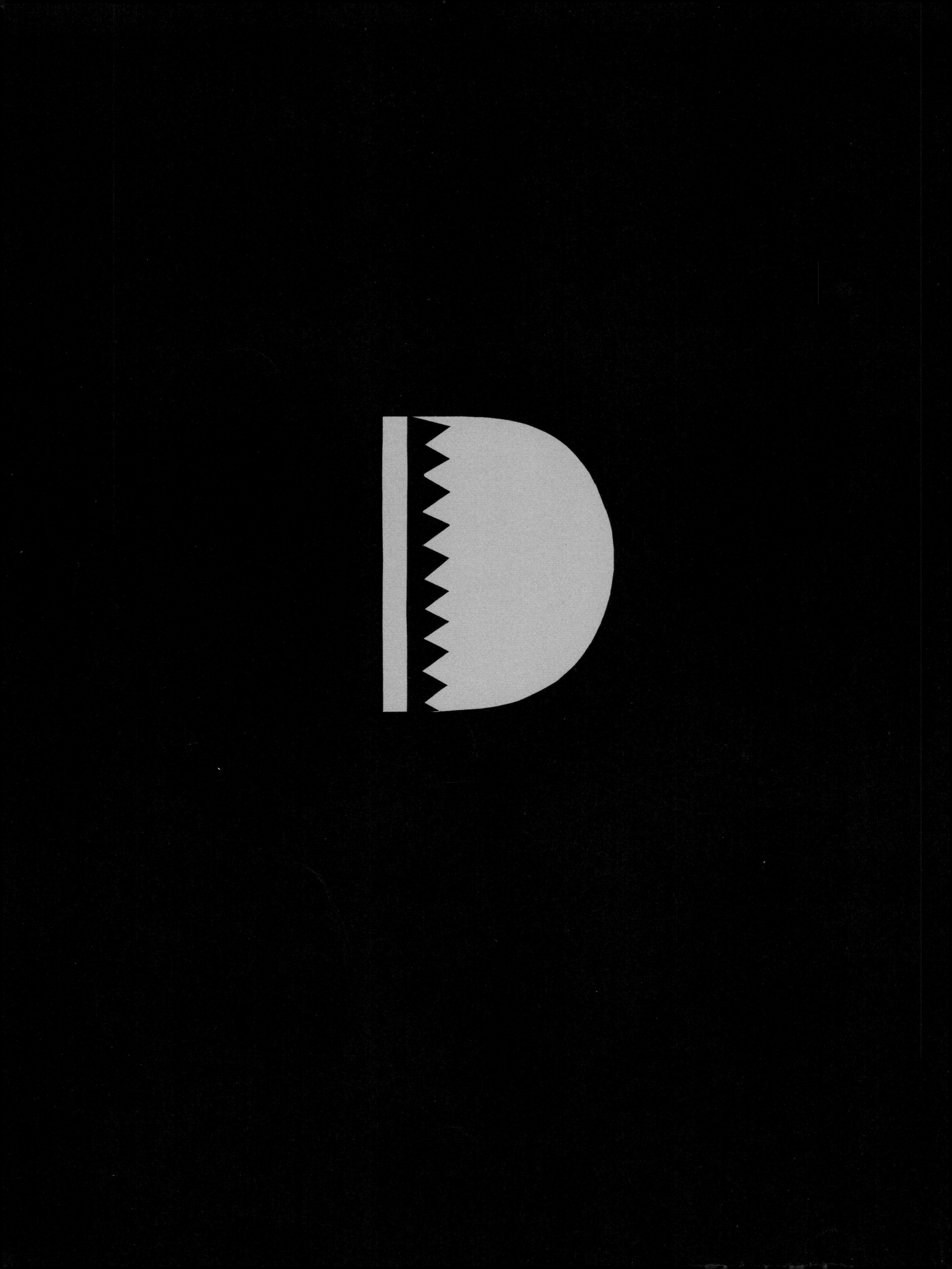

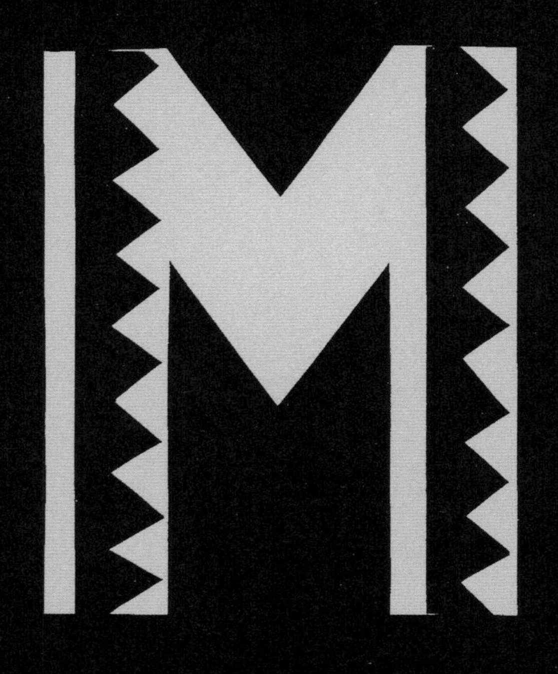

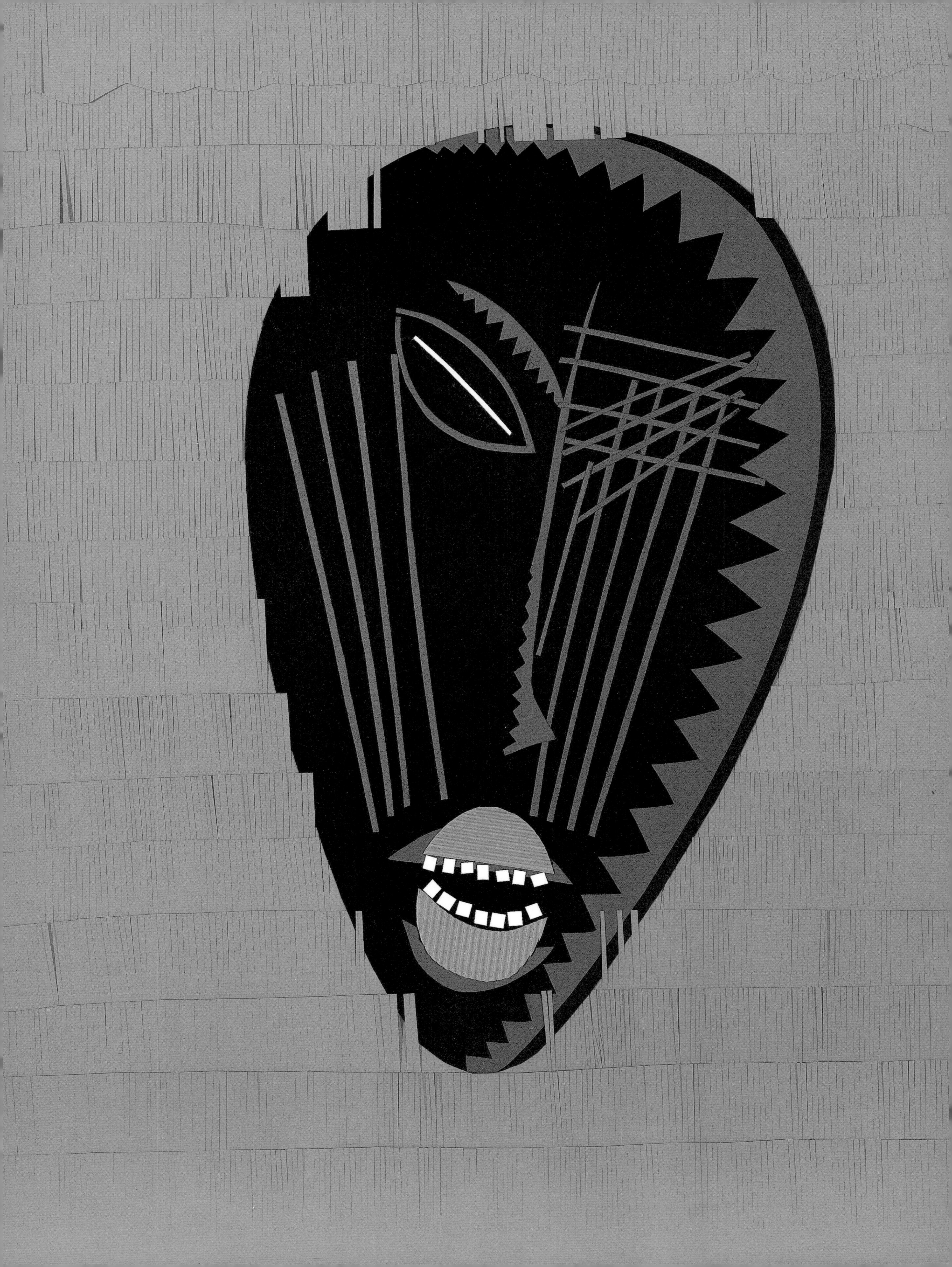

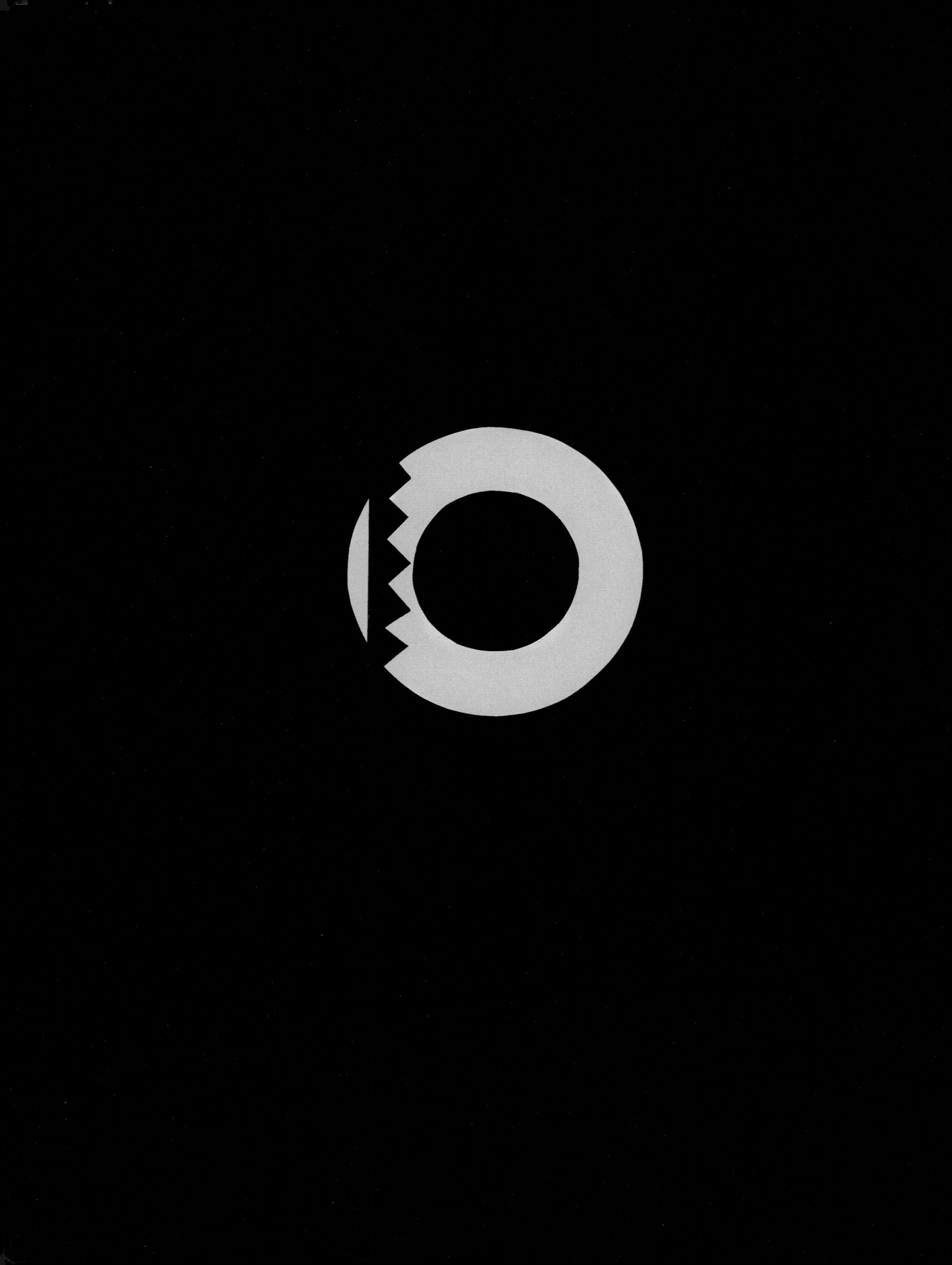

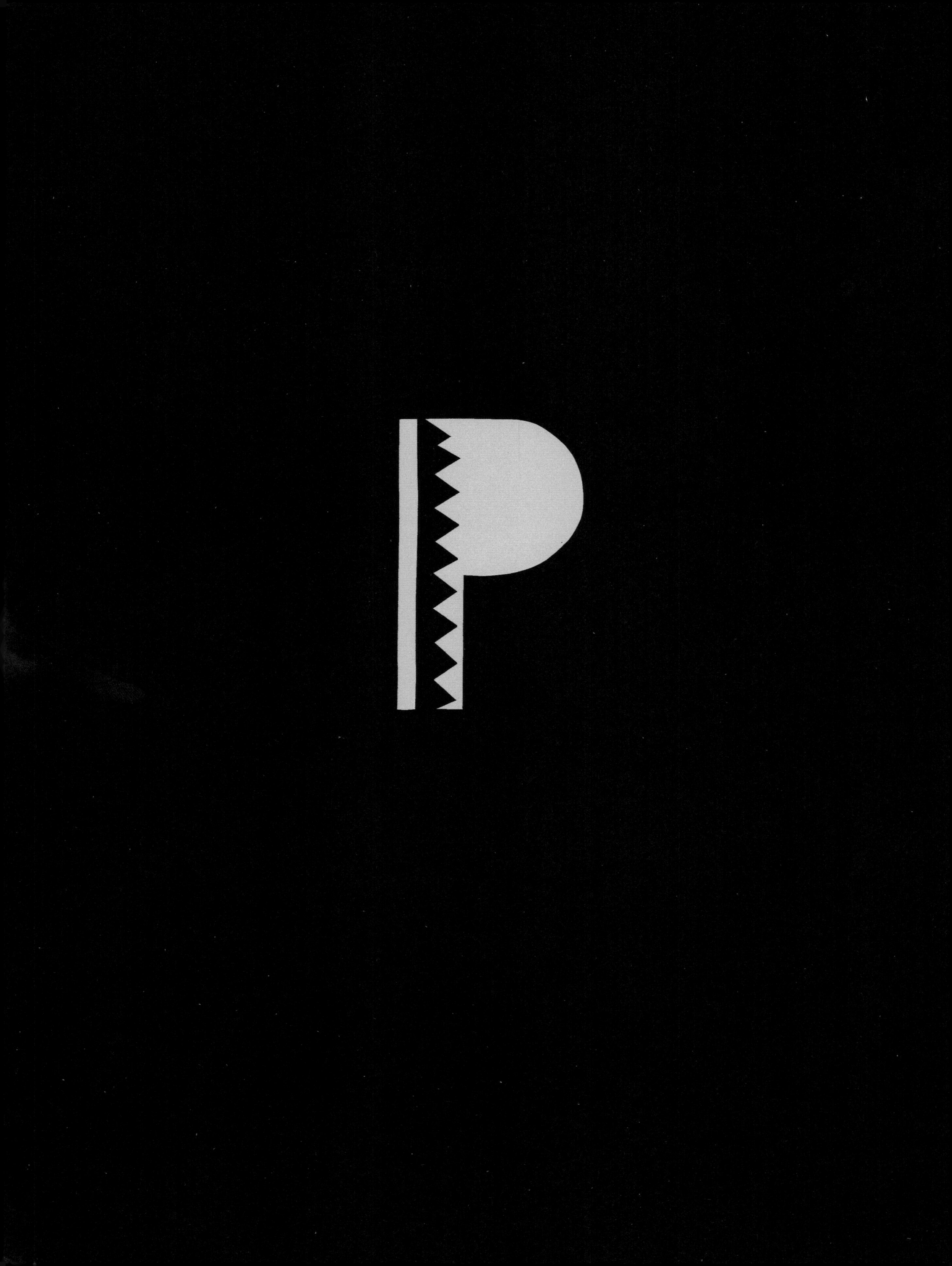

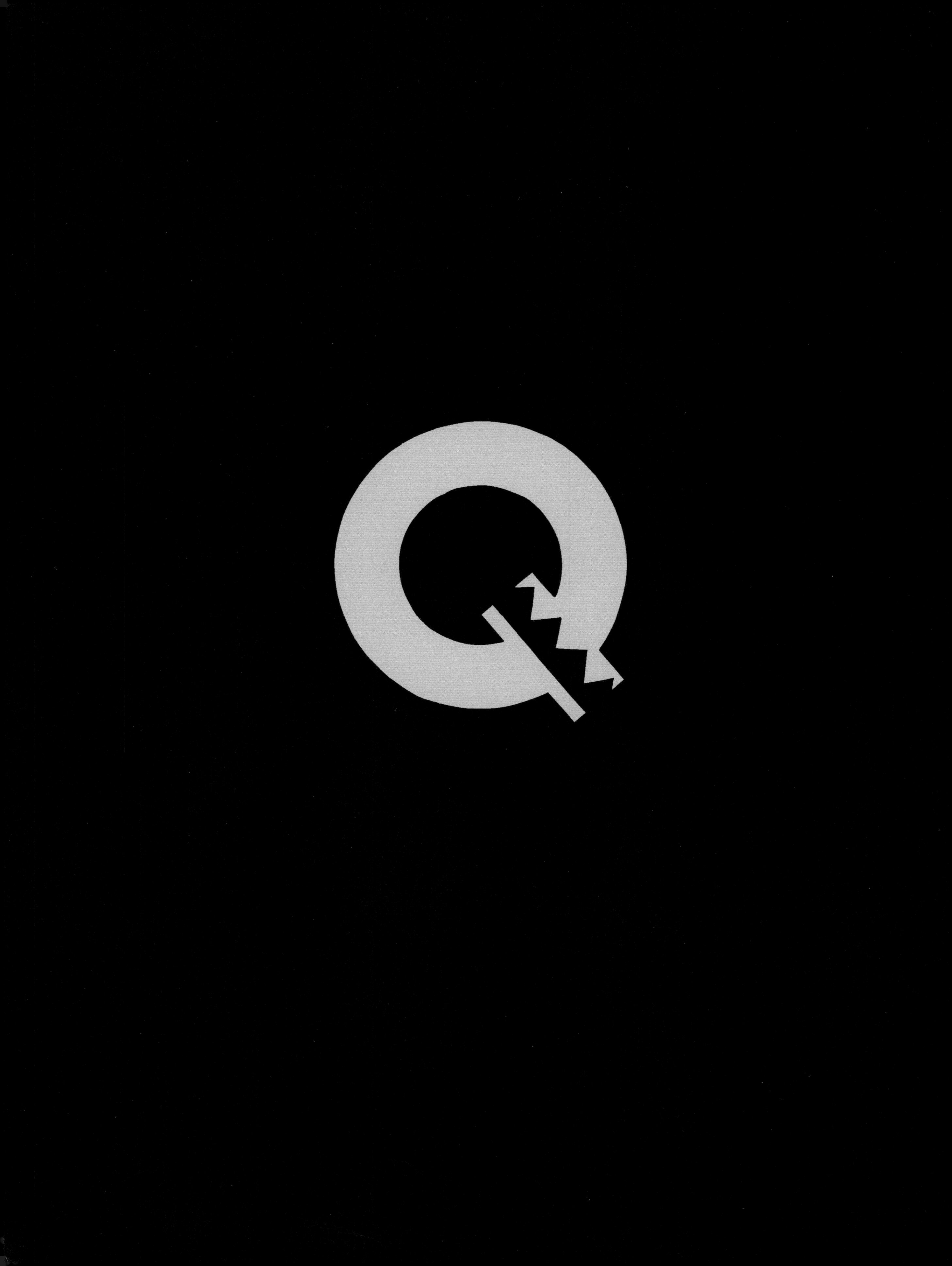

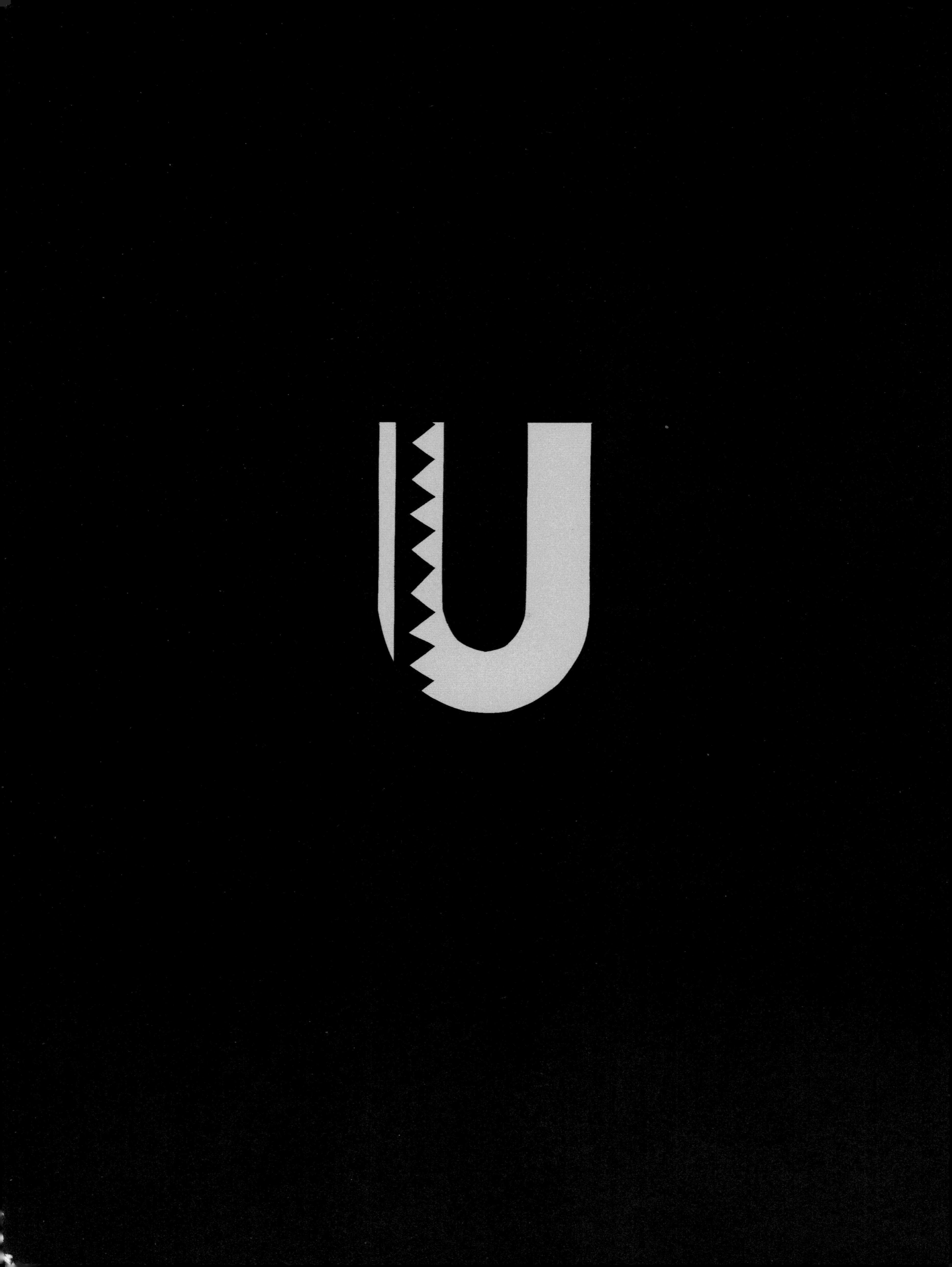
U

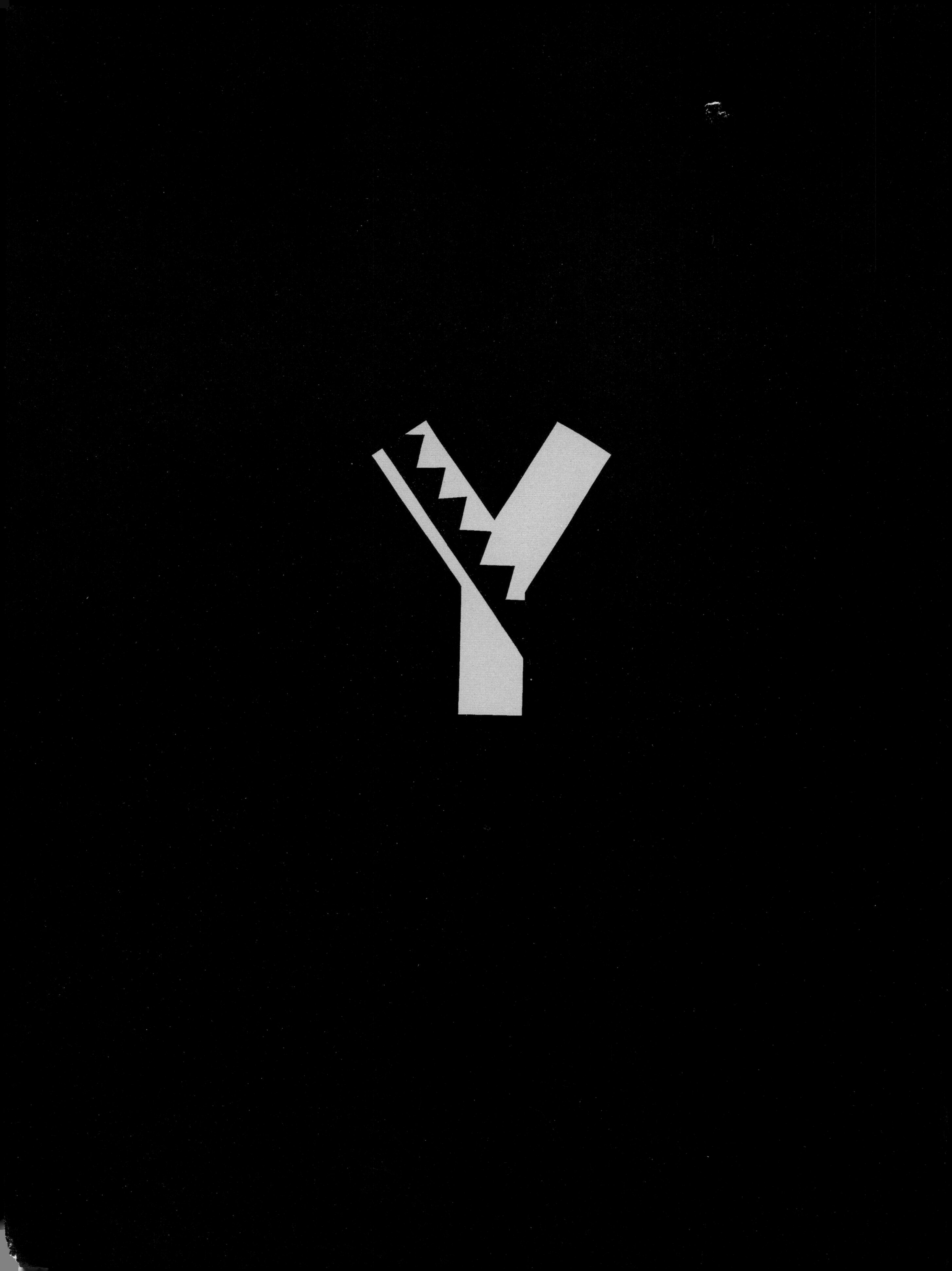

ANTELOPE
BANANAS
CHAMELEON
DRUMS
ELEPHANT
FIRE GIRAFFE
HIPPOPOTAMUS
IMPALAS
JUNGLE KRAAL
LEOPARD MASK

NIGHT ORCHIDS
PARROTS
QUEEN
RHINOCEROS
SNAKES TRIBE
UMBRELLAS
VASES
WILDEBEEST
XYLOPHONE
YAMS ZEBRAS

ABOUT MICHAEL ROBERTS

MICHAEL ROBERTS is a British fashion journalist. He is the fashion and style director of *Vanity Fair* magazine. He has worked as fashion director for *The New Yorker,* fashion editor of *The Sunday Times,* style director and art director of *Tatler,* design director of British *Vogue,* Paris editor of *Vanity Fair,* and editor of *Boulevard* magazine. He has also worked as a fashion photographer and illustrator, contributing images to publications including *Vanity Fair; L'Uomo Vogue;* British, Italian, French, American, Chinese, Brazilian, and Japanese *Vogue; The Sunday Times;* and *The Independent* on Sunday.

In addition to *Jungle ABC,* he has published three books of illustrations: *Mumbo Jumbo* (Callaway, 2000), *Snowman in Paradise* (Chronicle, 2004), and *The Snippy World of New Yorker Fashion Artist Michael Roberts* (L7/Steidl, 2005), a collection of his illustrations. Roberts also collaborated with creative director Grace Coddington to art-direct and edit *Grace: Thirty Years of Fashion at Vogue* (Steidl, 2002).

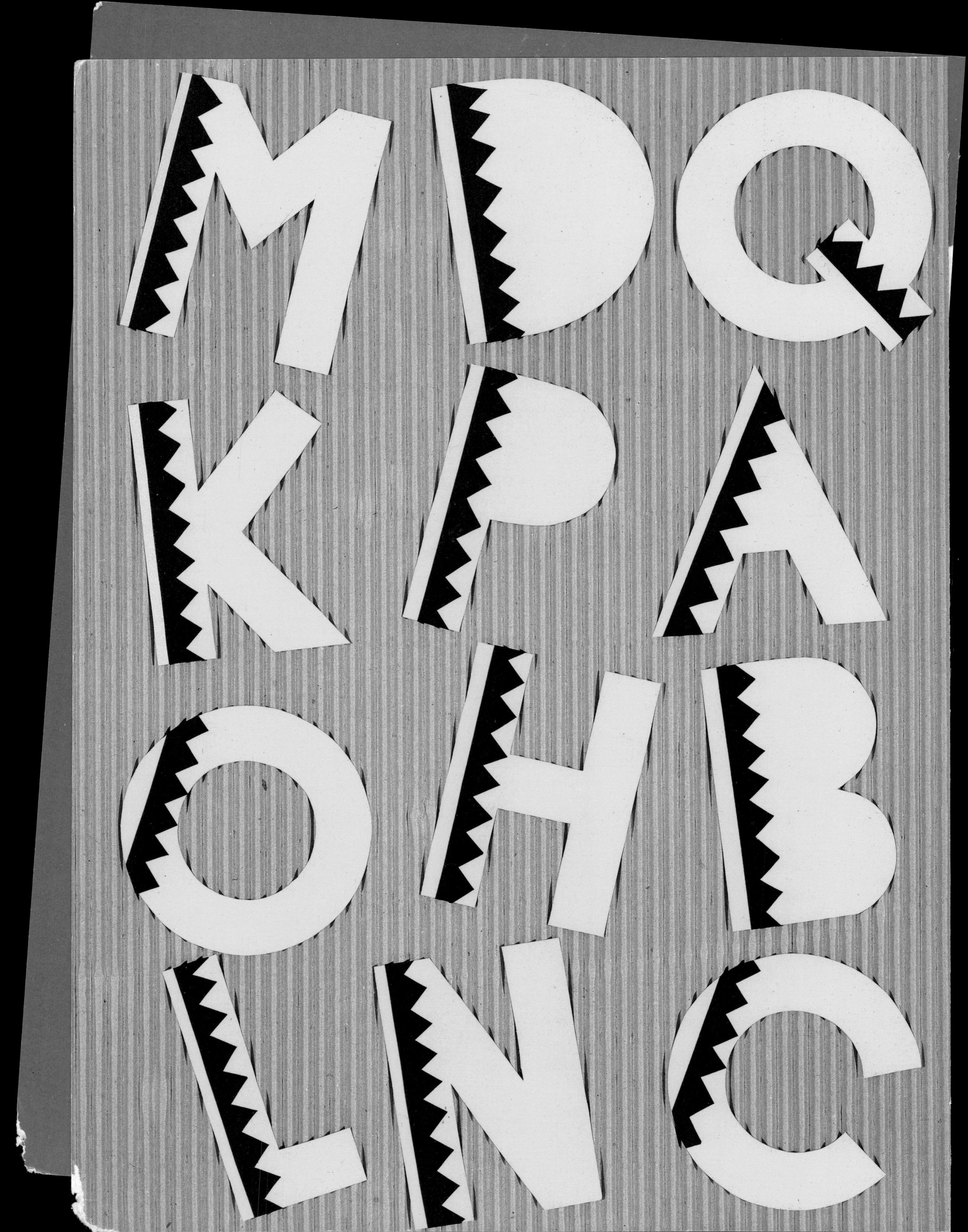
MDQ
KPA
OHB
LNC